Mc

by Mc

Cory was a normal sort of a guy and life was easy. Then Susie came from the future. She was beautiful. She was deadly. She wouldn't take no for an answer.

Other books by Martyn Godfrey

In **Series 2000**
(published by Collier Macmillan)

The Last War

In **Series Canada**
(published by Collier Macmillan)

Fire! Fire!	*Ice Hawk*
Spin Out	*The Beast*
Wild Night	*Rebel Yell*

Other titles:

Alien War Games
Here She Is, Ms Teeny-Wonderful
It Isn't Easy Being Ms Teeny-Wonderful
Plan B Is Total Panic
The Vandarian Incident
You Make a Great Girl, Mike!

series

2000

MARTYN GODFREY

More
Than
Weird

22227
WILLOWWOOD
SCHOOL

Maxwell Macmillan Canada

Copyright © 1987 by Maxwell Macmillan Canada Inc. All rights reserved. No part of this book may be reproduced or transmitted in any form or by any means, electronic or mechanical, including photocopying, recording, or by any information storage and retrieval system, without permission in writing from the publisher.

Maxwell Macmillan Canada

ISBN 02.953499.2

General Editor: Paul Kropp
Series Editor: Sandra Gulland
Designer: Brant Cowie
Illustrator: Greg Ruhl
Cover Photography: Paterson Photographic

Printed and bound in Canada

Canadian Cataloguing Publication Data

Godfrey, Martyn
  More Than Weird

(Series 2000)

ISBN 02.953499.2

I. Ruhl, Greg.   II. Series   III. Series

PS8563.033M67 1987 jC813´.54 C87-093926-2
PZ7.G62Mo   1987

To all the students who shared a classroom with me. Thanks for the laughter and inspiration. May the title always describe you.

CONTENTS

CHAPTER 1

Six months ago, I was an average teenager. And I mean that word—*average*. You couldn't find a guy more average than me.

I had a beat-up Toyota that was held together by wire and hope. At school, I had a lot of C's, with a couple of B's in Auto Shop and Drafting. I had zits, not a lot, but enough to worry that they might turn my face into a pepperoni pizza. My parents hassled me, enough so that I could complain about them to my friends. You see, I was just like you. Joe Average from Dawson Creek.

And then Susie came along.

My friend Chuck and I were eating lunch in the school cafeteria. It was cold for November, more like January. I was wondering if my Toyota would even fire up after school. That's when a beautiful girl walked past the caf windows.

She was so pretty. I mean, she was like right out of a video. Every feature on her face was perfect. Blue eyes, tiny nose, pouting lips, even the way her long blond hair swirled over her eyes. And her body? Well, let's just say that it *really* fit together.

And the weird thing was, she was dressed in a halter top and jeans. It was below freezing outside and she was dressed as if it was July. The cold didn't seem to bother her at all.

I watched her walk through the front doors of the school.

"Your trap's wide open, Cory," Chuck said.

"Huh?"

"You look stunned. What you looking at?"

I blinked and stared at him. "There was this girl—this *beautiful* girl."

"Where?" Chuck looked out of the window, too.

"She was wearing a halter top," I went on.

"In this weather?" Chuck laughed.

"You're seeing things."

I didn't have to prove it. The caf all of a sudden became quiet. That's something that never happens.

The girl was standing in the doorway. She was looking around the room, carefully checking each table.

Closer up, she was even more gorgeous. I figured that a girl just couldn't get any better looking. And so did everyone else, I guess. They stared at her like they didn't believe it, either.

"Is that her?" Chuck asked.

"That's the one," I mumbled.

"I'm in love," Chuck said.

The girl's eyes came to rest on our table and she checked out the two of us. First Chuck—and then me.

Then she smiled as if she had found what she was looking for. She walked toward us. Even her walk was perfect. Her head was thrown back so that her hair swayed as she moved. Her back was straight and she sort of . . . bounced . . . with each step, if you know what I mean.

Chuck jumped out of his seat. "Watch this move," he whispered. "Big Chuck is going to wow her."

Big Chuck is right. My friend was the captain of the senior football team. He was the nose tackle, and I don't think any team ever tried a line plunge through the centre.

Chuck stood between two tables and blocked the girl's path. She stopped in front of him.

"Out of my way," she ordered. Her voice was soft and smooth, but there was a hint of a threat in the tone.

"Hi there," Big Chuck grinned. "You must be new to the school. Allow me to offer my services as an escort. I mean, let me show you around the place."

"Out of my way."

"That's no way to make friends," Chuck said, still grinning.

She reached out her hand, grabbed his shirt collar, twisted it, and lifted him off his feet.

It was just like you see in movies. She held Chuck above her head with one hand.

His feet dangled in mid-air.

"That's impossible," I gulped.

And most of the people in the caf agreed. All around me I heard gasps and whispers of surprise.

Chuck's eyes were bulging from his head. His face had turned tomato red.

She heaved him to the side, the same way you'd throw your binder on the kitchen table. Chuck went crashing down on top of somebody's lunch.

I couldn't close my mouth. I was too stunned. She walked over to me and looked at me as if she was checking out each pimple on my face.

"Are you Cory Johnson?" she said.

I nodded.

"Good." She had a pleased smile. "You may call me Susie. Finding you was easier than I thought. I have come for you, Cory Johnson. I have travelled 550 years to come for you."

CHAPTER 2

Chuck moaned and swayed to his feet. "How'd you do that?"

"Who are you?" I asked.

But she didn't bother to answer our questions. "Cory Johnson, I need to talk to you. Is there some place we could go?"

"Me?" I mumbled. "Why do you want to talk to me?"

"It is most important," she went on. "We must talk."

Chuck was rubbing his rear end. He was trying to get a peanut butter sandwich off his jeans. "How'd you lift me up like that?" he wondered.

"We can go for a ride in my car," I told her.

"Cory?" Big Chuck squeaked. "You can't do that. This girl is dangerous. Let *me* take her for a ride. Give me your keys."

"No way," I protested. "It's me she wants to talk to, not you."

"Let me go with you, then." He winked.

I shook my head. "There isn't room."

"Come on," he said. "We've had nine people in your car."

"No room," I repeated. "Besides, Susie said that she wants to talk to me—alone." I smiled at her. "Isn't that right? Just you and me?"

"Correct," she nodded. "I wish to talk to you alone."

"I still think you should take me along," Chuck begged.

He was probably right. But I couldn't turn down the chance to be alone with such a gorgeous girl.

And let's face it, I was curious. That's the truth. I wanted to know who she was and what she wanted. I mean, she had hurled 100 kg of football lineman aside as if he was a Kleenex. And that was just another thing that made her interesting.

"She only wants to talk," I whispered to Chuck.

"Where is your car?" Susie asked.

I stood up. "It's in the parking lot. You'll really like it." I took Susie's arm to lead her back out the door. "It's a real fine machine," I bragged. "It's only ten years old."

Everyone was watching as we walked out of the caf. A few of the guys in my home room started hooting and banging on the tables. I knew they were wishing they could be me. Oh, what luck, I grinned.

"You're going to miss Auto Shop, Cory," someone called.

So what! I thought.

I wished I had a big beast of a car to impress her with. But she didn't seem to be too upset crawling into my old Toyota. The cold engine started in a cloud of blue smoke on the third try.

"Aren't you cold?" I said. I wondered why she wasn't shivering like me. "I think there's a blanket in the back. It's a little dirty, but it's warmer than what you're wearing."

Susie looked puzzled as my car coughed

and sputtered to a stall. I cranked it again.

"Needs a tune-up," I said. Susie nodded her head as if she believed that my car wasn't on its last legs.

I was going to head down to the local drive-in and treat her to a burger. But Susie had a better plan. "Is there a place we can go where no one will bother us?"

"Well, there is a place where the kids go when they want to . . . when they want to make out."

"That will be fine," she nodded.

All right! I thought.

It took a few minutes before the first hint of warm air hissed from the heater. But Susie didn't complain. She sat looking at the trees we passed at the sides of the road.

"It is strange to see so many trees," she said.

"Yeah, sure," I agreed. Maybe she was from the prairies. "You sure you're not cold?"

"I am fine," she said. "I have been formatted for your climate."

"Huh? What do you mean?"

"I was made so that the cold does not bother me."

"Made? You know, you sure are weird. In a nice way, that is. Dressing like that. And throwing Chuck around. And saying that you come from 550 years away."

"Cory Johnson, I *am* from the future," she said with a straight face.

"Yeah, and I'm from Mars."

"Pardon? Has there been some mistake? You are the Cory Johnson born at St. Mary's hospital on July 6th?"

"How'd you know that?" I stopped her. "This is a joke, right?"

"Good," she nodded to herself. "It would be a mistake to take the wrong person."

She studied me for a moment. "Cory Johnson, I come from the world 550 years in the future. You will like it."

"Sure," I laughed as I turned off the highway onto a gravel road.

"Two centuries ago, the last human travelled to the stars," she told me. "We wish to establish the species again in one of our zoos."

I laughed.

She stared at me. "Why did you make that noise?"

"Huh? What noise? I just laughed."

And then, as if all this talk wasn't weird enough, an even weirder thing happened. Her eyes went out of focus as if she was thinking. It was like a computer doing a memory search.

After a few seconds she refocussed. "Laugh," she said. "To make the sounds and movements of the face and body. Those that express lively amusement." Then she paused and looked puzzled. "Why do you find it funny that we wish to bring you to the future to be in our zoo?"

"Sounds like a sci-fi movie," I grinned.

"But it is true," she said. "Humans are not logical!"

"This sure beats Auto Shop," I told her.

"Before humans left the planet Earth, they invented robots," she went on. "Robots that could think and do the work that humans had once done. The world was a wonderful place for you humans. Robots

20

did all the work. No disease. Even death had been beaten."

"Sounds great," I agreed.

"But there is something in you humans. Something that is not logical. Some of your species continued to think. One day, someone found a way of flying huge ships out of your solar system. It became *the* Great Adventure. Over the years every human left to see what life was like in distant space."

"Everyone?"

She nodded. "Why would your species leave when they had everything?"

"The grass is always greener," I noted.

"Pardon? What does it have to do with the colour of Earth cover plants?"

"It's a saying. You know, the grass is greener on the other side of the hill."

"Not logical," she said. "Just like leaving the Earth to us."

"Us?" I laughed. We were way outside of town and she was still keeping a straight face.

"My model has been around for two

centuries." She seemed really proud of that.

"It's a great model," I replied.

"But now that we have solved the time movement problem, we wish to have a human on display. In a zoo, of course."

"Of course." I laughed again. "The time movement problem? Does that mean time travel?"

She nodded. "It has been a project for years. We saw it as a way to bring a human to our time."

"Why?" I grinned.

"So we can study you. After all, your species created us."

"O.K., get real. Who put you up to this? I bet it was Chuck, huh? Chuck is behind this, right? That's why you were able to push him around so easily. It's a great joke. I really like it."

"I am not joking, Cory Johnson. I have come to take you to the future. You were picked to be our prize display. Your name is already on the cage at our zoo—Cory Johnson."

CHAPTER 3

I laughed again. Susie looked at me with a tight frown. "Perhaps the computer was wrong," she said. "You seem simple-minded."

"What?" I stopped laughing. "What kind of put-down is that?"

"When we found out that we could bring a human to our time, we went to our master computer. We have, on file, records of all humans born during the last six hundred years. We asked the computer to scan those billions of people. We needed the person who would be best for our display."

"You're good," I said. I was beginning to smile again. I pulled the car to a stop at the end of the dirt road. At one time, the road led to a gravel quarry. Now it led to a spot for some late night togetherness.

"Of all those billions, the computer

picked you," she went on. "You are the most average person in the memory banks. You are a perfect display for the robots of the future to view."

"Wow," I smiled. "The most average, huh? What a loser! That's a terrific story. It can't be Chuck. He couldn't think up something so . . . so off the wall. Was it Pete? Did Pete plan this?"

"Pete?" she said. "You believe that I am not telling the truth?"

"Right."

"It does not matter. You will come with me, Cory Johnson," she went on.

It had to be Pete. He was into weird sci-fi things. And it was a good joke. In fact it was great. Pete must have searched real hard to find such a good-looking girl. Maybe he even paid her to do this. But what the heck? At least I had got a chance to talk with her. If I played things right, I just might be able to get her to go out with me.

"Sure, I'll go to the future with you," I said. "I'll go anywhere you want. How about to the show this weekend?"

"Good," she said. "We will go to the time gate right away."

"The time gate?" I asked.

Susie had missed my come-on. She was still playing the game.

"To allow us back into the future," she told me.

I tried to hold back my grin. "Where is this time gate?"

"Turn the car around and drive back to your school."

I could just see driving back into the parking lot. Pete and everyone laughing at me falling for the joke. I couldn't help it. I had to laugh.

"No," I said. "I'm not going to fall for that one. I don't want the guys to think I got suckered in on this."

"I do not understand."

"Look, Susie, you can stop now. The joke's over. Maybe you and I could grab a burger on the way back. What do you say?"

"Are you saying you do not wish to travel to my time?"

I nodded. "Of course I'm saying that."

"Cory Johnson, I have been programmed to take you back."

The way she said that, in her flat, smooth voice, made me shiver. I shifted in my seat. "Why don't we call it off now, huh? I mean you almost had me going."

"This is most puzzling," she declared. "I will have to scan my options."

Then she went into the "search" look again. And that was the first time that I felt some doubt—that maybe all of this wasn't a put-on. That maybe it was just weird enough to be true.

It took about ten seconds for her to rejoin me.

"Cory Johnson, if you will not agree to go . . . ."

"Come on, Susie," I said. "Enough."

"I will have to take you."

Quickly, she reached over and placed a finger against my temple.

"Hey, what are you do . . . ?" I started. But I couldn't finish. There was a high-pitched whine in my ears. Then a relaxing

feeling moved around my neck and down my spine.

"Hey," I said again. The one word sounded like a whole sentence. I was talking in slow motion.

"You will find this pleasant," Susie said. "I am closing down your central nervous system."

"Yeah," I giggled. "This feels goooood."

What was I saying? What was happening to me? How could she do this? I should have been scared.

But I wasn't. It was like all my muscles were floating against my skin.

"Alll rrriiiggghhhttt," I mumbled.

"There will be no damage to your body," Susie explained.

"Thhhaaattt'sss fiiinnne," I laughed. "Juuussttt fiiinnne."

It felt like I was in a water bed and the sides were growing around me. My eyes filled with a pleasant blue fog. And then, I wasn't anymore.

CHAPTER 4

I was aware of the blue fog again. It lifted slowly and my eyes came into focus.

What was going on? What had happened? A memory of something. Susie? Beautiful? Zoo?

Zoo? A girl from the future . . . no, a something from the future . . . was the girl a robot? . . . my head . . . she touched my head . . . and I was weird . . . .

Everything looked fuzzy. Was I in the future? I focussed on something. It looked like the glove compartment of my Toyota. The glove compartment door hung half off. I could see empty chip bags inside. That was disappointing. The future was the same as the present. Five hundred and fifty years and I still had to drive a beat-up Toyota.

"Cory Johnson," I heard a voice say. "Are you awake?"

Susie? I turned my head. Susie was sitting in the driver's seat next to me. She was trying to start my Toyota. I wasn't in the future. This was my car!

"I am glad you are awake," she said. "I am having trouble with the drive of this vehicle. I wanted to dispose of your car and move us through the time gate before you woke up. But I cannot start the engine."

She turned the key again and the Toyota let out a low grinding noise. She'd never get it started. The old wreck had a mind of its own. You had to hold the clutch halfway and floor the gas. If you didn't, the car would just moan forever.

"Tell me how to put it in drive," Susie ordered.

"Why should I?" I wanted my voice to sound tough, but it came out with a croak.

She turned the key again. More whining. "This is odd," she said. "I have been formatted to understand these motors. It is a gasoline-powered internal combustion motor, is it not? What am I doing wrong, Cory Johnson?"

My head cleared enough so that I could think. An idea came to me. "It's not a gas engine," I lied. "It's run by nuclear power."

"I do not understand," she frowned. "Nuclear power was not used until . . . ." Then her eyes blanked out again and there was this weird whirring sound.

And that meant she wasn't watching me.

I heaved myself across the seat and yanked the handle of the driver's door. At the same time, I butted my shoulder into her ribs. The door flew open and Susie went hurtling onto the gravel road.

I scrambled over the stickshift and got in the driver's seat. Then I pressed the clutch halfway, the gas full, and listened to the motor fire up.

Susie was on her feet as I pulled the shift into first. My tires sprayed gravel in the air. Susie grabbed the door as I began my U-turn.

"Wait," she ordered.

I floored the gas as Susie ripped my door off! She tossed it aside and grabbed at the Toyota. She caught the back bumper with

her right arm as I tried to pull away.

The car stopped. The wheels were spinning gravel and sand, but I wasn't moving.

"I have come for you, Cory Johnson," she shouted above the noise of my rear tires. "You cannot get away."

"That's what you think!" I shouted back.

I dropped the gas, threw the trammy back into first, and blasted the gas again.

I saw her stagger, but she didn't let go. It was like a tug of war. The car would move a little and then it would stop and dig more gravel.

Susie's right arm was stretched straight out. She was going to stop my car with one hand!

"Let go!" I swore. "Let go of my car!"

The Toyota stalled and I quickly threw the key and popped the clutch. And suddenly, I was fishtailing away from Susie.

I glanced in the mirror. Susie was bending over to pick something off the road. When I saw what it was, I almost drove the car into the spruce trees.

Her right arm had pulled off. Metal parts were hanging from it.

Susie's face had no expression. There was no pain, no anger, just a blank stare.

"Come back, Cory Johnson," she called as she calmly snapped her arm back on. "You cannot escape. I will always find you. You cannot escape . . . ."

CHAPTER 5

The wind howled through the empty car door as I headed back to town. I drove as fast as my old Toyota could go.

But where *could* I go?

Susie said she'd find me.

I was lucky to get away this time. But if she found me again . . . .

I couldn't go back to school. That's the first place the robot would look.

Or my house. If Susie knew my name and when I was born, she must know where I live.

How could I ask the police for protection? If I told the cops they'd think I was crazy. "Hi guys, I want you to protect me from this girl from the future."

"Right, buddy, we got just the room for you. It's got rubber wallpaper."

What a mess!

I glanced at my watch. Still another hour until school got out. Who could I turn to? Nobody would believe me.

I pulled into Chuck's driveway. His parents wouldn't be home until six and they kept a door key under the mat. I'd wait there until Chuck got home. Chuck was such a practical guy. He'd know what to do.

An hour and a half later, I was sitting at Chuck's kitchen table. I watched him put a whole package of salami on a sub bun.

"You sure you don't want something to eat?" he asked.

"Eat! Why would I want to eat at a time like this? I want help. Don't you believe me?"

He sat down at the other end of the table. "Sure. I believe that foxy piece of fluff was a robot. I can dig that, Cory."

"You don't, do you? You think I'm just making it up."

He admired his sandwich. "Well, to tell the truth, it seems like a crazy story. Why don't you just admit you struck out?"

"I didn't strike out!" I snapped. "I

escaped. Look at my Toyota."

"I always wondered how the door stayed on as long as it did," Chuck said as he bit into the sub.

I grabbed his arm. "Chuck, I'm not joking. I've never been more serious. She's a robot. I heard the whirring inside her head."

"Maybe she was really turned on," he winked.

"She snapped her arm back on!" I shouted. "When she touched me, she made this strange feeling go all through my body."

He placed his sandwich on the plate and wiped his mouth with the sleeve of his sweater. "I used to feel that way in grade eight when I was going out with Barbie. You remember Barbie, huh?"

"A real doll," I hissed.

"And then there was Cathy," Chuck went on. "Why, I remember one time when she was—"

I banged my fist on the table, making the sandwich bounce on the plate. "Susie made me pass out!"

Chuck looked at the sub for a second,

then at my fist, and then at me. "You're *really* serious."

"Yeah," I nodded. "I need help."

"Cory, it's such a weird story."

"I know it is."

"More than weird."

"Yeah," I agreed.

"You sure you haven't been dropping a few pills? I mean . . . ," he paused. "You and me go back a long way, Cory," he announced. "And even if you are cracking up, I'll still help you."

"Thanks," I said. "I think."

"Let's go tell the cops," he suggested.

"Think about that," I pointed out.

He did for a moment. "They'd throw away the key." Chuck waited, thinking harder. "Then you'll just have to tell your folks."

"Can you imagine what my dad would say?"

"I guess you don't need that," he agreed.

We sat in silence for a few moments.

"I got it!" he smiled. "Run away."

"Sure," I nodded. "Just take off."

"No." He jumped up from the table and opened the drawer under the sink. He pulled out a key ring and removed one of the keys. Then he handed it to me.

"This is for our summer cabin at Seba Beach," he explained. "Everything is closed up for the winter. Nobody is out there. You'll be safe from the robot." He scratched his hair. "Did I really say that? Oh, well. You remember how to get there?"

"Sure," I answered. "But what am I going to tell my folks?"

"Leave it to me," he said. "When my father comes home, I'll tell him you phoned me and told me this stupid story . . . ."

"Stupid?"

"O.K., this believable story. And I'll say that you're going to hide out for a few days. I won't tell anybody where. Then my dad and I will go tell your folks. No doubt, they'll think that you've . . . I mean, they'll call the police and ask the cops to check out Susie. Sound good?"

I shook my head. It sounded downright stupid. Almost as stupid as the truth I was asking my best friend to believe.

I had no choice.

I put the key in my pocket. "Thanks, Chuck."

He picked up the sandwich again. "No sweat, Cory. If a robot was after me, I know you'd do the same thing."

CHAPTER

I was tired and cold when my car plowed down the hill to Chuck's family cabin. There was a lot of snow in the bush and I wasn't sure if I'd be able to drive out. Oh well, I had nowhere to go anyway.

The cabin had shutters up for the winter and I didn't take off any of the boards. It seemed more of a hideout that way. I turned on the power and fired up the propane heater. There were a couple of boxes of Kraft Dinner in the cupboards. I threw the macaroni into a pot and turned on the stove.

After eating, I curled up on the couch and tried to get to sleep. But I ended up thinking of Susie and what had happened hours before. It seemed so unreal, as if it had happened to someone else. I wondered how my parents were taking it. Chuck would have told them by now.

When I woke up, it was daylight. Thin ribbons of light shot through cracks in the shutter. I stretched. My head ached. Then I remembered.

I swore and swung my feet onto the floor. The light painted bright strips across the old carpet. It was almost too bright to look at.

But then the light vanished for a moment. The room went suddenly dark.

When I realized what had happened, my stomach cramped. "Oh, no!" I whispered. Somebody was outside! Somebody had walked by the window and blocked the light.

Who was it? The cops? Maybe Chuck told them where I was. No, Chuck was stubborn. He wouldn't give in and he wouldn't go back on his word.

But maybe Chuck did tell my parents where I was. Maybe it was my mom and dad coming to take me back home. No, if Chuck did bring them out, they'd just knock.

Or maybe it was someone who lived nearby. Maybe they saw my car and came over to check it out. Hardly. This was strictly a summer place. All the other cabins were summer places as well.

The ribbons of light disappeared again. I heard a shuffling outside the window. Someone was trying to look in. Could they see me in the darkness?

The sunlight returned. I tried to hear footsteps, but I couldn't.

When the front door began rattling, I almost jumped off the couch. I watched the door handle jiggle back and forth on the locked door. The handle jiggled hard and the door banged on its hinges. Then there was silence.

I waited, not moving. Maybe if I didn't make a noise whoever it was would go away.

There was a loud knock on the door. "Cory Johnson," a girl's voice called. "Cory Johnson, open the door. I will talk to you."

That was the "maybe" I hadn't wanted to think about.

"Cory," she called. "Open up. I know you're in there."

There was no doubt about it. It was Susie. I'd never forget that voice.

I eased myself to my feet and crept into the kitchen. I slid the top drawer open as quietly as I could. I felt around for a thick handle and pulled out a weapon.

Groan! A soup ladle! I put it gently on the table and searched for something else— but there was nothing.

Susie kept tapping at the door.

"Cory, you will let me in," she said.

I grabbed the soup ladle and turned toward the door. It was the only weapon I had. My legs turned oozy all of a sudden and I had to go to the bathroom. Oh, super. A robot is trying to take me to the future and I had to pee.

There was a pounding on the door. "Cory!" Susie hollered. "This is important. I will speak to you."

I clutched the soup ladle and waddled on my shaky legs back to the living room.

"Go away!" I squeaked.

Susie's voice brightened. "I will not harm you, Cory Johnson," she promised. "Open the door. Let me in."

"Fat chance," I called.

I ran into the bathroom. Even when there is a robot after you, you still got to do what you got to do.

Susie was banging even harder on the door. "Cory Johnson, you will open this door."

Feeling better, I returned to the living room and watched the door bounce with each powerful knock. I backed up. Better not to get hit with a flying door.

"I have a weapon," I said, looking down at my soup ladle.

"A weapon?" she asked. There was a silence and then that strange whirring sound. "What is a weapon?"

"I have a . . . knife," I lied.

It took Susie a few seconds to answer. "You do not need to harm me. I will not hurt you."

"Right," I called. "Just like the last time."

"I have made a mistake in my plan," Susie said.

"Huh?"

"I will talk with you," she went on. "I

47

will not hurt you."

"We can talk through the door," I said.

"It is important," she went on.

I sighed. "We have nothing to talk about. I don't want to go through a time gate thing. I don't want to live in a zoo. I don't want to live in the future. Living in the present is hard enough."

A short silence. "I will tell you how wonderful it will be."

"How nice," I told her. "But I still don't want to . . . ."

The door exploded. The wood cracked and split into a spray of splinters. Susie walked through the smashed door with her index finger held out.

I swung the soup ladle at her and it bounced off her head with a ping. She stopped for a moment and regarded the ladle with interest. "Is that a weapon? Is that what humans of this century fight with?"

I pinged it off her head again.

"Most curious," she said as she pointed the magic finger at my face.

I went backward, tripping over the coffee table. As I tried to get my balance, Susie pressed her finger against my head.

And the feeling washed through me again. My mind fell into the blue fog.

CHAPTER 7

It was like an instant replay of what happened in the car. I tried to stay awake, but I didn't have the strength. Susie pushed me backward onto the couch.

"You silly human," she scolded. "Why do you not believe me? I said I would not harm you."

Slowly the blue fog burned away. I could see Susie sitting beside me on the couch.

"I made a mistake trying to force you to come with me. Now I will tell you how wonderful it will be for you."

The cold air from the open doorway made me shiver. "What are you talking about?" I tried to shake the fuzz from my thoughts.

"I will use another means to get you to the time gate," she went on.

"But I won't go," I pointed out.

Susie threw her head back and waves of blond hair flew across her face. "You are so silly. But what can one expect from a human?" And then she laughed. A high, songlike laugh. It was perfect, just like her looks.

She touched my hand. Her skin was soft and warm! "You have taught me to laugh— just like a human. Does it sound right?"

"Not bad," I had to admit. She was awfully cute—for a robot.

"This time I want to *invite* you to the future," she explained.

I shook my head. "No way. I don't want to be a monkey in a zoo."

She laughed again and the sound of it tingled my spine. She slid over next to me on the couch. "I am told that human teenage boys like this," she explained. "Is it true?" she asked.

I didn't know what to say! "Uh . . . yeah," I stammered.

"Interesting," she said, moving closer. "But let me explain, Cory Johnson," she went on. "It is not a cage as you know it.

Imagine it to be a world full of all the things you've ever wanted."

"Except a door marked *exit*," I said.

Susie rubbed her finger along my bottom lip. "Don't look like that," she smiled. "It makes funny little wrinkles on your face. And put on your jacket. You look cold."

I did as I was told.

"That's better," she smiled. "You really *are* cute for a human. I want to invite you to join me in the future. You don't have to live here anymore," she went on. "We can give you a world that is a paradise."

"Huh?"

"A place where anything you'd want would be yours. Think of it."

"Anything?" I grunted.

She nodded. "We could even make you so you would never die."

"Never?"

"*Everything* you've ever wanted." She leaned toward me. "Forever and ever . . . ."

"Would . . . would *you* be there?" I mumbled.

"If that's what you want. I can be

programmed to do anything that you want. I can do anything that a human female can do." Her voice came out low and raspy and I had to catch my breath.

I pulled away from her. "You know, this is all kind of hard for me to grasp. You know what I mean?"

She nodded and closed her eyes and brought her face close to mine.

And then I heard the whir again. Something inside her head was spinning. Some piece of metal or plastic or whatever. Something that wasn't *real.*

I was getting turned on by a machine!

I jumped up.

"Stop that," I snapped.

She smiled again. "You're so cute when you get mad."

"Look," I said. "I can't leave here. I've got my family and friends. I can't just follow a robot through time."

"Why not?" she asked.

"Good point," I nodded.

"I'm offering you everything you want. In return, all you have to do is smile at a few curious robots for a couple of hours a day."

"Just smile?"

She laughed again, way up high and sexy. "That's all. You *do* want to come, don't you?"

I had to admit I was really thinking about it. Having anything I wanted had a few good points.

"Sit down again, Cory Johnson. I want to get to know you better. Much better."

I looked at her, at her face and her *everything.* What did I have to lose? She was really quite a sexy . . . machine!

That was it. That was the problem. She wasn't real. As soon as I got close to her I'd hear the whir of her gears.

"Why don't you want to be happy?" She batted her long eyelashes at me.

"I've got reasons," I told her. "Look, back in the Toyota you were going to take me whether I wanted to go or not. How can I trust you?"

She raised one eyebrow. I had this picture of Mr. Spock trying to figure out my logic.

"That hurts, Cory."

"Don't give me that," I said angrily. "Stop acting like a person when you're a machine! I'm not stupid!"

Again, she raised her eyebrow.

"I can tell what you're trying to do," I said. "You're coming on all sweet and . . . ." I ran out of words.

She smiled.

"And you're offering me all these things. Everything I ever wanted. But it's all a bribe."

She nodded. "There is nothing wrong with that."

"You're tempting me, but how can I believe you?" I said. "How do I know you won't take me to the future and stuff me?"

"*Stuff* you?" She looked puzzled. "I don't understand."

"There's no way that I can know that you're telling the truth," I pointed out.

She broke into a wide grin. "Wait, Cory Johnson. There is a way."

CHAPTER 8

Susie lead me from the cabin. I followed her to the edge of the lake and onto a cement boat dock.

She looked around. "This will be a fine place to set up the time gate."

"The time gate?" I asked suspiciously.

"It is not a trick, Cory Johnson," she told me. "The time gate will allow you to see the future—to see the wonderful world that waits for you."

That didn't sound right. Maybe she could set up the time gate thing. Then what would stop her from just pushing me through? I backed away.

She smiled. "It is just as they told me. Humans are suspicious. I have already said that I will not trick you, Cory Johnson."

Sure, and I'm supposed to trust a robot that ripped the door off my car.

I looked at the ice on the lake. It stretched almost to the middle, but it wasn't that thick. Not thick enough to walk on, anyway. If I needed to escape, I'd have to run back to my car.

"The time gate isn't really a gate," Susie told me. "It's a point where time and space exist as a singularity. Do you understand?"

"Sure," I lied. "I'm into that stuff."

She undid her belt and took off the buckle. "This is a temporal pulsar. It will create a small warp. Once it appears we will have a window to the future."

"Of course," I nodded.

Susie placed the buckle-pulsar on the ground. It began to vibrate. The air above it started to wave like it was above a fire. There was a slight hum in the air.

"It is the gate," she told me. "In a moment, you will be able to see my time. Rather, you will see *our* time."

I stared at the fuzzy air. I could see blurry shapes in the haze.

"It will only take a few moments." She smiled.

"Is it open now?" I asked. "If we walk into it, will we be in the future?"

"Yes," she nodded. "We can pass through any time."

One of the shapes in the fuzz was moving.

I looked at Susie. She sure was a good-looking girl.

But no! She wasn't a girl at all. That was what I'd been fighting all along. I'd been seeing and not seeing. The bottom line was —Susie was a machine.

"Susie," I went on, "acting real nice was just a way to get me close to the time gate, wasn't it?"

The smile vanished from her face. "I meant all those things, Cory Johnson. We will make you happy. I will make you happy."

The moving shape in the fuzz was female. Even though it was out of focus, it looked an awful lot like Susie.

I had to do something in a hurry. I couldn't stay around this time gate thing much longer. Susie would just zap me with her wonder-finger and I'd be history.

Then again, if I could push *her* through the time gate . . . .

But what was to stop her stepping back to get me?

And then I glanced at the ice.

"Susie," I asked, "what makes you tick? I mean, where do you get your power from? Do you have to eat?"

She smiled at me. "That is a strange question."

"I guess I'm kind of strange for someone who's so average, eh?" I told her. "Do you have batteries inside?"

She nodded. "It is similar to that."

And most machines run by batteries don't work all that hot when they're wet, I thought. *They short out.*

"O.K.," I said. "I'll go with you. You don't have to blue fog me again."

She nodded. "That is a wise choice, Cory Johnson. I knew that if I told you how good it is going to be, you'd agree."

Susie held out her hand. "Take my hand, Cory. We will pass through the time gate together."

I looked at her hand and then at the lake.

I reached out my hand toward her and stopped. I looked over her shoulder. "Oh, no," I gasped loudly. "We have company!"

There was no one there, of course, but Susie twisted around anyway. And as soon as she did, I charged at her. I butted her ribs with my shoulder.

She staggered off balance and fell to her hands and knees. But my tackle hadn't sent her off the dock! She was getting back up as I threw myself, head first, at her shoulders.

There was a loud smack as my head met her metal body. A bunch of stars bounced in my vision and it was my turn to stagger. In the corner of my eye I saw Susie waving her arms to try to keep her balance. There was a whir of motors as she tried to correct herself.

And then there was a loud splash.

Rubbing my head and still wobbly, I edged to the end of the dock. There was a large hole in the ice. A lazy stream of bubbles came up to the water's surface.

The bubbles became smaller and at last

the surface was still. I looked into the green murk. Nothing.

I looked back at the time gate. It was humming loudly and the shape on the other side was clear. It was another Susie. Only this time she was dressed in a blue metallic jumpsuit. I looked at her and she looked back at me.

And for a moment there, just a few seconds, I almost stepped through the gate. A chance to spend the rest of my life with a machine that looked like that . . . .

But it was the word *machine* that stopped me. I picked up the buckle-pulsar. There was a raised star shape in the middle. I pushed at it, but nothing happened.

"Is that you, Cory Johnson?" the Susie from the other side called.

She was almost completely in focus. Could she step through and get me?

I twisted the star and the time gate sizzled and vanished in an angry pop.

I looked back at the point where Susie had splashed into the lake. A piece of brown algae drifted to the surface. And then another piece. And then another.

Something was moving down there.

I shoved the buckle thing into my jacket pocket and ran for my car.

CHAPTER

I had to get away from Seba Beach. It was a mistake trying to hide out by myself. I had to get into a crowd. Susie couldn't drag me through a time gate if there were other people around.

I dove into my car, pulled the keys from my pocket, and cranked the Toyota. True to form, it coughed and sputtered to a couple of stalls.

And then it died!

A low, grinding groan was all my poor car would offer. After two more tries, there was nothing, not even a click.

"Great!" I swore. "Just terrific! Make my day."

I got out of the car and kicked the fender. "Thanks," I shouted. "I treat you nice, take you to the car wash a couple of times, plug you in when it gets cold. I even changed your oil last summer. And what do you do? Die on me when I need you most!"

And then it dawned on me what I was doing. I was talking to my car. I was talking to a machine.

I glanced back at the dock. I think I half expected to see the other machine I'd been talking to. But Susie hadn't surfaced. My plan must have worked. The water must have shorted her circuits.

That algae. It was as if something was moving around on the bottom . . . .

It was 15 kilometres back to the town of Seba. I needed a sweater under my jacket if I was going to walk that far. And it would be smart to get some kind of weapon, just in case.

I ran back to Chuck's cabin and found one of Chuck's ski sweaters. It was far too big for me, but it would be warm. And then I searched for something that would stop a robot—a rifle, maybe. Both Chuck and his dad hunted and I hoped that they left their guns in the cabin. No such luck.

I did find a screwdriver, though, and that

let me break into the cabin next door. Again nothing.

I broke into another cabin. Still nothing.

By the time I broke the lock on the fourth cabin, it dawned on me that I was running for my life. I was trying to stop a robot from zapping me 550 years into the future!

Now, don't think I flipped a breaker, but I started to laugh. Not just laugh, but *laugh!* I fell on a bed and laughed until my guts hurt. It was so stupid.

I read somewhere that the things which happen in life are really strange. You only have two ways to deal with them without losing your basket. You laugh or cry. I guess I was coping real well.

Another cabin. Don't people keep guns out in the open anymore? What's this country coming to?

In the next cabin I got lucky, a single shot .12 gauge shotgun. But I couldn't find any shells. I searched every drawer and cupboard with no luck.

"Freeze!" a voice called.

"What?" I turned my head.

"Drop the gun! Now! Put your hands on your head!"

Standing in the open front door of the cabin was the town cop. He had his legs planted apart and he held his .38 service special with both hands.

"Drop it!" he shouted.

I let the shotgun fall gently onto the carpet.

"Hands on top of your head!" he ordered.

I did as I was told. The cop was overweight. His parka couldn't hide his large belly.

"Look, sir," I began. "This is not what it looks . . . ."

"I can see what it is," he snapped. "I followed your trail. You're in trouble, boy."

"You think I've been robbing these places?" I smiled at him. "You think I was going to use this shotgun? I just found it. It's not even loaded. Look, I'm not the bad guy, honest. I'll tell you the whole story after we get out of here. Let's leave right away."

"Why are you in such a hurry?" he puzzled. "There someone else here with you?"

"No," I answered. "Not really. Well, not a person anyway. I'll tell you after we leave."

"Tell me now."

"It's kind of silly," I said. "I'll tell you at the station."

He squinted his eyes. "Why are you in such a hurry to get out of here?"

"Do I *have* to tell you now?"

He nodded.

I sighed. "There may be somebody after me," I told him. "She may come out of the lake to take me to the future."

"What you been smoking, boy?" he said with a chuckle. "You aren't making a whole lot of sense. What do you mean *she?* You got a girl with you?"

"She's not really a person," I explained.

"She's not a girl?"

"She's from the future," I said. "She's a robot."

He gave me a stern look. "I don't want to hear any more. Now let's go check the other cabins and find out why you really want to leave so fast."

One last try. "I realize that you think I'm a looney-tune."

"You said it!"

"Well, I'm not. I'm just a normal, everyday kid."

The most average person of all time, I thought. "And I'm caught in this nightmare that is right out of a movie. But I'm being completely serious when I say a robot's after me."

"Now you take it easy, boy. Everything's going to be O.K. I'm gonna slip on these cuffs and we're gonna check the other places. You understand?"

"Wait," I said. "I can prove it's the truth. I've got the key to the time gate."

"The what?"

"It's in my pocket. It's from the future and it'll . . . ."

"Enough!" the cop snapped. "I don't want to hear any more of that bull."

"Just look at it," I pleaded. "How's that going to hurt?"

The cop flicked his .38 a couple of times. I figured that meant I could take the buckle-pulsar from my pocket. "Slowly," he warned.

I held it up for him to see.

He took one hand from his gun. "Pass it here."

He looked at the thing as if he expected it to explode. "It's just a belt buckle," he snarled.

"No it isn't," I said. "If you turn that star, it'll open up a doorway to the future."

And that's what he started doing with his thumb. "I can't believe you, boy. This is the stupidest . . . ."

"Don't!" I shouted.

The air beside him began to sizzle and crack. It turned fuzzy and again an out of focus shape moved within the blur.

"What the . . . ." the cop gasped.

"Turn it off!"

"Hello, Cory Johnson." A voice spoke from behind the cop.

The cop wheeled around. There stood Susie, hair hanging down in wet rat tails.

Pieces of algae clung to her.

"Cory Johnson—I have come for you," she said. Her eyes showed purpose. This time she knew what she had to do—and nothing was going to stop her.

CHAPTER

The cop looked at Susie, then at the wavy air, and then quickly back at me. He seemed frozen, like he wasn't sure what he was supposed to do next.

Who could blame him? He was watching a time gate to the future while holding a gun on a half-wit. And then a gorgeous wet robot appears. That's enough to make Rambo feel ill.

The cop's voice was shaky. "Get your hands on your head like your boyfriend. Then get over here," he ordered Susie.

Susie looked at him the way she looked at Big Chuck in the school caf.

"I said, get over here!"

"She's come to take me to the future," I said. "That's why she's here. And she won't let you stop her."

Susie looked at me. "That was a foolish

thing you did, Cory Johnson. That could not stop me. You will come with me."

"Shut up, both of you!" the cop ordered. "You think you got a nice little gig here, huh? Do the job on the summer places. You didn't think I patrol around here, did you? Well, you can't fool me by acting crazy. I'm gonna bust your rear ends to the moon. Now, listen here, girl. Hands on your head and get over there next to your boyfriend!"

"I have come for Cory Johnson," Susie said. "I do not want to harm you."

"What . . . ?" the cop sputtered.

"Shoot her!" I said. "Shoot her!"

The cop looked at me. "Are you—"

"If you don't, then she'll take me!" I pleaded.

"I said . . . ," he mumbled.

"Look at the gate!" I dropped my hands and pointed at the wavy air. "There's another robot."

Through the fuzz, I could see another Susie. "That's 550 years from now."

The cop stared at the time gate with an open mouth.

"Please shoot it," I begged. "I don't want to go."

Susie walked calmly toward him, but he was too stunned to act. She reached out and placed her finger on his forehead.

"Too late," I groaned.

The cop's eyes went glassy. "Oh yeah," he said. "That feels great. That feels so good. How are you . . . ? What are you . . . ?"

Then his eyes rolled up in his head and he began to sway on his feet. Susie pushed him away from her.

He fell back, the gun still in his hand. As his shoulder bashed the wall, his right arm flew forward.

THWACK!

The shot made me flinch. And it made Susie jerk. There was a neat bullet hole in the false skin of her neck.

She watched the cop slump to the floor. Then she began to sway as well, first one way, then the other. There was a buzz of something inside her, then a wisp of smoke from the bullet hole.

She faced me and staggered forward. I backed up and watched her legs buckle. She smashed onto the cabin floor.

I ran over to the cop and grabbed the pulsar from his hand. I twisted the star and the time gate vanished with an angry pop.

The cop had this stupid grin on his face. "You're going to be all right," I told him.

He mumbled something that made no sense.

I turned toward Susie. I bent down beside her and listened. She wasn't making any noise. I stared at her face. The eyes were closed and she looked so peaceful, just like she was asleep. Then I looked at the bullet hole.

"Does this mean you're dead?" I whispered. "Or broken? Or whatever happens to robots when they switch off?"

She still looked beautiful, but more like a store dummy than a real girl. I didn't have to remind myself that she was a machine.

"Where . . . ?" the cop groaned. His eyes opened slowly. "Where am I? . . . It's so blue."

He focussed on me. "What . . . ?" Then he saw Susie. "Oh no," he gasped. "I killed her."

"No, you didn't," I said. "She's not a person. Come and take a closer look. There's no blood."

He staggered to his feet and moaned. He stumbled, put his hand on my shoulder, and stared at the bullet hole in her neck. "There's wires in there," he said.

"Right," I agreed. "Like I said, she's a machine."

He looked at me stupidly. "Where's that fuzzy air?"

"I turned it off."

"Right," he nodded. "Why not?" Then he looked at the robot again and put his gun back in the holster. "Let's get out of here, boy."

The cop's 4x4 was parked at the bottom of the hill. I climbed in the passenger side as the cop got into the driver's seat.

He rubbed his eyes. "I've never felt like that before," he said.

"I know," I agreed.

"This is weird. No—it's more than weird. No one will believe this."

Again, I agreed.

He turned the key and I looked at the cabins and cottages. What a quiet, peaceful place for such things to happen.

And then I saw her! Susie! She was coming toward the 4x4. Her voice was weak, but I knew what she was saying. "I 'ave 'ome for you, 'ory, 'ohnson."

CHAPTER

You should have seen that cop race his truck up that hill. He slipped through those gears like he was in the Indy 500. But when you're being chased by a robot you don't want to hang around.

I told the cop the whole story and he believed me. How could he doubt it? He'd seen Susie return from the dead. But, so far, I think he's the only one who *really* believes me.

The RCMP didn't move too fast after we got to Dawson Creek. In fact, I thought they were going to take the cop and me to the psychiatric ward. Not that I can blame them.

When they finally sent a cruiser out to Seba Beach, Susie was gone. And I haven't seen her since.

The RCMP weren't too thrilled by my

break-ins. They charged me with B and E. It never got to court, though. They gave me a lie detector test and it showed that I wasn't lying. When the crown attorney heard this, she dropped the charge.

But it wasn't because they thought I was telling the truth. As an RCMP guy told me, "The lie detector only shows that you *think* you're telling the truth."

"What about the Seba cop?" I asked. "He's crazy, too," the officer declared. The crown attorney said I had to go see a shrink. So for three hours a week, I talked to this guy about Susie. He kept asking me how I got along with girls. And if I had a thing for machines. Talk about crazy!

Anyway, I stopped seeing the shrink after five weeks. He told me that I'd imagined most of Susie. He said she was a real person and I'd made up a fantasy about her.

When I asked where she was now, he just pointed at my head.

Then I asked why the overweight cop saw her as well. He said, "You were able to convince him to share your fantasy."

Right!

My folks sure treat me differently. My mom is always feeling my forehead. Maybe she thinks I'm going to get a fever and start "seeing things" again.

Big Chuck wasn't too happy that Susie smashed the door of his folks' cabin. But at least he humours me. He says he believes that Susie really was a robot.

"You know, Cory," he said, "if it was me, I'd have gone with her. I mean, who cares if she was a machine? If she comes back, you send her to see me," he grinned.

"You bet, Chuck," I tell him. "I'll do just that."

I wonder if she'll ever come back. I sure hope not.

No doubt Susie got back to her own time and was repaired. Maybe she got a new program. If I was *from* the future, I'd send her back to find the *second* most average person of all time.

Maybe they've already found that person. Or maybe it could be you. Look, if you ever see this great-looking girl, then listen closely for the whir of motors.

You know, I often wonder what the future is like, and if I made a mistake. But I don't worry about it. You see, I've still got the buckle-pulsar thing. I didn't tell the cops about that. I figure that I might use it someday.

So if you ever hear that Cory Johnson has gone missing, then you know where I am. Or rather, *when* I am.

About the Author

Martyn Godfrey lives in Edmonton, Alberta, with his two children, Marcus and Selby. When he isn't teaching or writing, Martyn is often giving talks to students about writing. His first book, *The Vandarian Incident,* was written when a student in his grade 6 creative writing class challenged him to write. Martyn has lived in several areas of Canada, including the North. He has also lived in England.

Series Canada titles

by William Bell

Metal Head

by Martyn Godfrey

Fire! Fire! *Ice Hawk*
Rebel Yell *Wild Night*
Break Out *The Beast*

by John Ibbitson

The Wimp

by Paul Kropp

Hot Cars *Dope Deal*
Run Away *Burn Out*
No Way *Dead On*
Dirt Bike *Fair Play*
Snow Ghost *Gang War*
Wild One *Baby, Baby*
Spin Out *Micro Man*
Amy's Wish *Take Off*
Get Lost *Head Lock*
Tough Stuff

by Prem Omkaro

Nine Lives

by Sylvia McNicoll

Jump Start *Split Up*

Other titles in Series 2000

by Paul Kropp

Jo's Search
Death Ride
Not Only Me
Under Cover
Baby Blues
We Both have Scars
The Victim Was Me

by Martyn Godfrey

The Last War
In the Time of the Monsters

by John Ibbitson

The Wimp and the Jock
The Wimp and Easy Money
Starcrosser
The Big Story

by Marilyn Halvorson

Bull Rider

by William Bell

Death Wind

by Lesley Choyce

Hungry Lizards
Some Kind of Hero

by Dayle Gaetz

Spoiled Rotten

by Jennifer McVaugh

Hello, Hello;

Teacher's Guides are available for
Series 2000 and **Series Canada.**